From the Author

Writing this book scared me – here's why

I first wrote about Spencer in another book called *Diary of an (Un) Teenager*. Spencer is thirteen but doesn't want to be a teenager. So he decides he'll stay an (Un)teenager instead.

After I'd finished the book I worried what you'd think of Spencer. Would you think he was annoying – or just weird? No, you loved him. Spencer got fan mail. And at some schools I visited, pupils even dressed up as him.

And many of you asked me to write another book about Spencer. That's when I got scared. Everyone liked the first one so much, I didn't want the next one to be a let down.

So I spent ages just thinking about Spencer. I thought about Spencer at a school disco. I began to smile. And what would Spencer think of Facebook? Now I was laughing and couldn't wait to start writing this book.

And I really hope it makes you laugh too, whether you're meeting Spencer for the first or second time.

This book is for all the people who asked me to write another book about Spencer. Well, here it is.

Visit Pete's website:
www.petejohnsonauthor.com

Contents

Find out how it all started in

Diary of an (Un)Teenager

by

Pete Johnson

Chapter 1
The Real Me

Friday July 24th

4.20 p.m.

I shouldn't have done it.

But what else could I do?

"Soon be over," I said. And then I did it. I put on – a hoodie.

I looked at myself and I felt sick.

"Hey, you look cool, Spencer," said Zac, my best mate.

"No I don't," I muttered. "I look gross."

I had a baggy top on too. And skinny jeans with rips all over them. Why do teenagers buy jeans that are full of holes? They're mad, that's why.

"Well, move around a bit, then," said Zac. I'd put on my new hoodie in Zac's bedroom.

I took a few slow steps.

Zac laughed. "You're walking about as if you've got a suit of armour on. Just chill out and copy me." He had a hoodie on too. Then he started to strut about with his hands nearly touching the floor. He looked just like a gorilla.

"This is how you've got to walk tonight," said Zac, "when you meet any hot babes."

"I'm not interested in hot babes," I said.

"That's good, because they're not interested in you either," Zac snapped.

"You know I'm doing all this for just one girl," I said.

"I know," yawned Zac. "You love Emily."

I was thirteen last week and Emily sent me a birthday card with a heart on it. That was my first big surprise. The second one was that we then had two kisses which I enjoyed greatly. So did Emily. I'm very happy about that. But Zac said tons of other boys fancy her. So I can't hang about. And I'm going to ask Emily out at the school disco tonight.

Zac also said I can't ask Emily out in my normal clothes. He kept on about how she deserves better. So that's why I'm going to all this trouble. To please the only girl I've ever kissed – or ever wanted to kiss.

But it doesn't feel good. I feel ashamed.

That's because on my thirteenth birthday I made a promise I'd never change into that terrible of things – a teenager. I'm never going to bother about designer clothes and girls, and all the other terrible things that go with being a teenager.

But I've already let myself down very badly.

So once Emily says she'll go out with me, I shall be back in my normal clothes forever. I shall also tell her that I can't see her every night, because I've got lots of hobbies. And they take up a great deal of my time. But I will be only too happy to see her most Saturdays.

I shall tell Emily all this at the school disco tonight.

5.10 p.m.

I've spent all my birthday money and part of my savings on terrible clothes. So I expected my parents to go mad. But they don't. They looked shocked for a moment and then smiled.

"You're seeing Emily again tonight," said Mum, "aren't you?"

"Er, I might be," I said. I hoped I wasn't blushing. "How did you know?" I added.

Mum and Dad smiled as if they knew all my secrets.

"She's a nice girl," said Mum.

Dad agreed and then said, "When I was growing up, the Mods came back in fashion." He shook his head. "So I blew all my money on Mod clothes. But I had to have them."

And that's all they said about my clothes.

How dare they not tell me off? They're not acting like proper parents at all.

Later I heard Mum say to Dad, "Spencer's growing up fast."

That made me very cross. I'm wearing these awful clothes for one night only, and then I'm going right back to my old ways.

5.40 p.m.

I look around my bedroom at my computer games, my super-hero comics and all my model aeroplanes. It's such a great place to be. Somewhere you don't ever want to leave.

And I've never been to a school disco before. So I'm feeling a bit nervous about that. But I've got to look on it as an exciting adventure, like going into the jungle.

6.00 p.m.

I walked downstairs in my disgusting new clothes and then shot upstairs again. I'd just remembered something. Emily said she liked me because I'm "different from the others". Those were the very words she said. I can't go to a party looking exactly like everyone else. I don't think she'll like me any more.

How can I have been so stupid?

6.10 p.m.

I changed back very quickly. Now I'm wearing clothes that I like – a very smart, orange jumper which my nan kindly knitted for me. It's also got a matching knitted tie. I've put on my black school trousers – they go really well with the orange jumper.

It's so great to feel like me again.

6.30 p.m.

My parents looked very surprised to see me in my normal clothes again.

"You've changed, Spencer," said Mum.

"The other clothes didn't feel right," I said. "These do."

Mum and Dad didn't answer at first. They were so shocked, they couldn't breathe, I think.

Then Zac rang on the door-bell. "All right, Spencer?" he began, "ready to meet lots of fit girls …" Then he gave a sort of yell. "But what have you done to yourself?"

"I'm going to the party as the real me, and I'm not going to pretend to be someone else. This is my favourite jumper, you know." Then I added, "Everything comes back in fashion in the end."

"You'll have a long wait before that comes back in fashion," Zac said.

"You wore clothes just like this once," I said. And it's true, Zac did. "But then you got brain-washed," I went on.

"Spencer, go and put on the clothes we bought today," shouted Zac. "I don't mind waiting for you." He was almost begging me.

I think Dad must have been listening because he came out into the hall. "If you want to get changed, Spencer," Dad said, "I'll drive you and Zac to the school disco."

I gave him a hard look. "So, Dad, you'd rather I went to the disco in a hoodie, than in a very smart jumper and tie. Just what kind of a father are you? We don't want a lift, thank you."

Dad hung his head and didn't say another word. He just went back into the front room and sat down again.

7.20 p.m.

Just before we got to the school Zac stopped. "You go on ahead, Spencer," he muttered. "I've got to ... do something."

"Do what?" I asked.

"Oh, just one or two things," he said, not looking at me.

"You're too embarrassed to walk in with me, aren't you?" I said crossly.

"No," he said at once and then added, "It's just there's this girl I like and if she sees me with you ..."

"She might think we're mates," I said. "And you don't want her to think that, do you? You don't want to talk to me at the disco either."

Zac shook his head slowly.

"But," he said, "I'll talk to you on the phone tomorrow, for as long as you like. And good luck," he called after me. "You'll need it."

7.25 p.m.

Once men fought dragons to win a girl's heart.

I'm going to a school disco.

I'd so much rather face a dragon.

Chapter 2
At the School Disco

7.40 p.m.

I nearly didn't go into the school.

I almost ran home.

But then I thought again of Emily. And I so wanted to go out with her – on Saturday nights.

So I kept on walking. And it was great to see a friendly face – Mr Wells, my English teacher. He was sitting at a table, just outside the school hall, to check the tickets. It was odd to see him in a T-shirt and jeans and not in his normal grey suit. He looked very shocked to see me.

"Oh, Spencer, this is a big surprise," he said.

"Well, I thought I'd drop in," I smiled.

"Good for you ... and I hope you enjoy yourself," he went on. But he didn't seem very sure about this.

At first I didn't think anyone else was in the hall. There was a very colourful ball hanging on the ceiling (a disco ball I believe it's called). It was going round and round and sending out all different colours – over no one at all.

But then I saw I wasn't alone. Only everyone was standing together on the edges of the hall – boys one side, a few girls on the other.

"Good evening," I said to a boy in my class. He didn't answer, just stared hard at me as if he'd seen a monster.

"No way," he gasped at last. Then he prodded some of the boys next to him. They all started to laugh so hard one of them began to turn bright red. Soon every boy there was killing themselves laughing – except Zac. He was smiling too – but in a highly embarrassed way.

7.50 p.m.

This boy has just strolled into the disco, with sun-glasses on. I mean, how daft is that? His name's Oscar and he really loves himself. Yet no one seems bothered he's wearing sun-glasses at night, in a disco. He hasn't had one funny comment.

But the boys can't stop pointing at me. And they're calling out stuff like – "Are you wearing those clothes for a bet?" and "Hey, Grandpa!" Another boy came up to me and shouted, "I'd rather eat a bowl of snot than wear that jumper," and then fell about laughing.

"Comedy genius," I muttered.

7.55 p.m.

About twenty girls have just arrived together – and one of them's Emily. She's wearing a blue dress and she's got a lot of jewellery on. She looks fantastic. And my heart gives a little jump when I first see her. She's standing with another girl. Her name's Jade and she's a show off and rude too. I wave and Emily gives a gasp when she sees me.

I want to go over and talk to her. But all of the other boys are staying on this side of the hall. They're just staring at the girls. It's weird.

8.10 p.m.

More people have arrived. But not one person has stepped into the middle of the hall. And I'm still stuck here with all the boys. But the mood has got very tense. There's a lot of whispering and nervous laughing, as if everyone's waiting for something to happen.

8.15 p.m.

Oscar, the boy in dark glasses, has just flicked a piece of chewing gum at Emily. It landed right on her cheek as well, making her jump. I was very angry. I was about to have strong words with him when Zac came over to me.

"Did you see that?" I cried. "Talk about rude."

Zac turned to say something to me but I could hardly hear him. "No, he wasn't being rude," Zac whispered. "Flicking gum means he fancies her."

"What!" I couldn't believe it. "Flicking a bit of chewing gum with spit all over it means he likes Emily?"

"Exactly," said Zac.

"Well, I'm not doing anything like that," I said.

"No, you just come here dressed as a ninety-year-old," snapped Zac.

"At least I don't have pretend holes in my jeans," I said. "And I keep telling you, Emily likes the real me."

"Someone has to, I suppose," said Zac. Then he grinned and I couldn't help smiling too.

"So when are we allowed to talk to the girls?"

"Things should kick off any minute now," said Zac. "And I'd ask Emily out before – he gets in there," he nodded at Oscar, "because girls like him."

"Not Emily," I said firmly.

"Got to go," said Zac. He went back to the gang of boys from my class. They'd stopped laughing at me. They were all looking at the girls now. And another boy was flicking chewing gum at a girl he liked.

Teenagers are very, very strange.

8.25 p.m.

At last!

A few girls have started to dance together in the middle of the floor. And some boys are edging towards them. At the same time, someone's put out all the food at the back of the hall.

And I see Emily walking towards the food. So here it is at last – my big chance.

Chapter 3
About Emily and *Dr Who*

8.40 p.m.

Emily and Jade were standing together with little plates of food.

I rushed over. "What's the food like?" I asked.

"Nearly as terrible as your jumper," replied Jade.

I pretended to laugh.

"Aren't you eating?" asked Emily.

"Oh, I will in a moment," I said. "But I had rather a big tea. Mum likes me to have lots of vegetables."

"How very interesting," said Jade. She was being extra rude to me tonight. And she was wearing tons of bangles which made a racket and clattered all the time. Still, she wasn't important.

Only Emily.

And I can normally talk to her so easily, but today I couldn't think of one thing to say. It must have been the jangling noise Jade's bangles were making. And Emily seemed to be in a bit of dream too.

"I think the weather's going to be good for the next few days," I said, at last.

"Oh, is it?" said Emily.

"Yes, no rain until at least Tuesday." I went on. "Maybe even Wednesday or Thursday if we're lucky. Still, rain is very good for the garden." I wanted to ask Emily out. But all I could talk about was the weather.

I tried again. "What I really wanted to ask you ..." I said.

Emily looked up. "Yes."

Now I just had to say one simple sentence – "Would you like to go out with me?" – but instead I gave this odd high squeaky cry. I sounded like a parrot. What's happened to my voice? All at once, it's out of control.

And then, before I could try and say another word Jade pulled Emily away – to talk to another girl.

"See you later," I screeched.

Emily did look back and I'm sure she nodded.

8.45 p.m.

I don't think Emily's enjoying this party any more than me. That's why she didn't say much. She and I have so much in common. I <u>will</u> definitely ask her out tonight. But first I just want to check on my voice.

8.54 p.m.

I said a few sentences out loud. And my voice seemed to be OK again. It was bad luck that three boys saw me talking to myself.

"Just making sure my voice is working OK," I told them. "It's really been playing up tonight. Does your voice ever do that?"

They just shook their heads and one muttered, "You are so weird."

Then another added, "What are you doing here, anyway?"

Friday July 24th

9.15 p.m.

At last I'm starting to enjoy myself. Just had a great chat with Mr Wells about *Dr Who*. He thinks the best ever *Dr Who* is David Tennant – but I said it was definitely Tom Baker.

Mr Wells was amazed that I knew so much about the Tom Baker days. "But they were made before you were born," he cried.

I said, "Oh, I have them all on DVD." Then I told him what my three favourite Tom Baker episodes were. And Mr Wells told me what his top three David Tennant episodes were.

It was the first proper chat I'd had all night. Mr Wells wanted to talk longer but he had to go and break up a fight. Two boys from my class had just started to attack each other. So Mr Wells sent them both outside for five minutes to "cool down".

At that moment, a Year Nine girl started to cry. And suddenly a group of girls were fussing all round her. I heard one say, "Oh, don't cry, Marie, he's not worth it."

Is anyone here actually enjoying themselves? I'm sure they'd all have far more fun watching Tom Baker as *Dr Who*.

9.25 p.m.

Zac is standing on the edge of a group of boys. He is sipping his drink and nodding along to the music. He keeps laughing too, even though no one is actually talking to him. When he isn't laughing and nodding he looks hot, sweaty and fed up. As I pass him he whispers, "Have you asked Emily out yet?"

"Not yet."

"Why not?" he asks me.

"Well, I've been talking to Mr Wells."

He turns and faces me. "Why?"

"Well, he's a big *Dr Who* fan like us," I say.

"But you don't come to a party to hang out with the teachers." Zac sounded shocked and cross. "Do you want to go out with Emily?"

"Of course I do," I say.

"Well, you know Oscar's been hanging round her all night ... You need to go and ask her out now," Zac tells me. Then he turns away from me and goes on pretending to enjoy himself.

Zac's right. But I feel very shy here. Perhaps if I invite Emily to join me outside? No, that doesn't sound right. What about if I say, "Emily, it's a nice summer evening with lots of stars in the sky. Would you care to look at the stars with me? I can tell you some of their names"?

No, far too long – but I'll think of something. And I just hope my voice works OK. It was fine when I was chatting about *Dr Who*.

I'm going to see Emily NOW.

9.45 p.m.

A massive set-back. I couldn't find Emily anywhere. So in the end I went up to Jade who was with a group of boys. Her smile froze when she saw me.

"Sorry to interrupt your fun," I said. "But have you seen Emily anywhere?"

"Emily's gone home," she snapped, "with a very bad head-ache." She said it as if Emily's head-ache was my fault.

9.50 p.m.

I slunk out of that party. I didn't even say good-bye to Zac.

9.55 p.m.

Did Emily just pretend to be ill? Did she really leave because she was unhappy?

Well, that's not my fault, is it? I hardly spoke to Emily – except to give her the weather forecast for the next few days.

I'm very sorry Emily didn't tell me she was leaving. Maybe I was talking to Mr Wells when she left. And she didn't want to interrupt our conversation. Yes, that was it, I'm sure.

10.05 p.m.

Not a very good disco – in fact it was a terrible one. But at least I didn't let myself down. I came in my own clothes. I was true to myself.

As for Emily ...

10.08 p.m.

I've just decided something. I'm going round to Emily's house tomorrow afternoon. And then I shall DEFINITELY ask her out.

Chapter 4
Shocking News

Saturday July 25th

3.45 p.m.

I'm feeling nervous but my mind's made up. I know what I've got to do. I ring the doorbell to Emily's house. Then my heart sinks as Jade opens the door. I just cannot get away from her.

I say, "Good afternoon, Jade, I'd like to speak to Emily, please."

"Well you can't," she says, "because she's not very well."

"Oh, I'm sorry," I reply. "What's wrong with her?"

"Do I look like a doctor?" she snaps.

I nearly tell her what she does look like – a very big-headed, totally annoying, extremely rude girl. But I don't say this. I ask, "Would you tell Emily I called and I'd like to see her soon?"

Jade looks at me for a moment, then says in a softer voice, "It's best if you don't call round here again, as Emily's going to be very busy. Bye then ..." she stops to remember my name.

"Spencer," I tell her.

"Bye, Spencer," she says and slams the door shut.

Have I just been dumped? I believe I have.

But it doesn't make sense. I mean, only last week Emily sent me a birthday card and put a heart on it. And since then we've kissed – twice. So what's going on?

I mean to go on to Zac's house, only I start walking up the wrong road. The shock's made me lose my memory. And I actually forget where Zac lives. So then I sit in a bus shelter and take some very deep breaths.

An old lady looks me up and down. "Are you all right, love?" she asks.

"I think I've lost my memory," I tell her.

"Oh, dear," she cries.

"Don't worry – it's rushing back now," I say and I get up. "That's a big relief."

"It must be," she agrees.

What if my memory had never come back? Well, I wouldn't have been able to go home for a start, because I wouldn't have had a clue where that was. I might have been lost on the streets for days ... all because of Emily.

4.30 p.m.

I've just told Zac everything. He didn't look very surprised.

"I didn't tell you before, but last night Jade told me ..." he waits and looks at me.

"Yes," I said, "Go on."

"Emily is seriously angry with you," said Zac.

"Why?" I asked.

"Guess," said Zac.

"Not because of what I wore ...?"

"I warned you," he told me, "not to wear those weird freaky clothes."

"But it was a party," I cried. "I thought you could wear what you wanted."

"And you can," said Zac, "only not that. You looked like a total joke last night – and made Emily look like one too. And now she's dumped you, hasn't she?"

I couldn't answer. I was in the grip of really strong feelings. Zac looked at me. "Don't take it so bad ... Emily's not that hot," he said.

"Yes she is," I answered back.

"So what do you like about her?" he asked.

"Everything," I replied.

Zac thought for a bit. "There is one thing you can do," he said and told me what that was. And I'm off to do it right now.

6.30 p.m.

Zac said I should buy her some flowers. So I did – twelve red roses. Not cheap, but I didn't care. I marched off to Emily's house with the flowers but I only got to the top of her road.

At the top of her road I saw the door to her house open and out came Emily – and Oscar. He turned round and put his arm round her. And they looked at each other in a very sloppy way as they walked up the road. I quickly ran off and I threw the roses into the first bin I saw.

Then I came home and had my tea.

9.45 p.m.

I told Zac what had happened and later he came round. "Come on," he said, "let's have a kick about." We went to the park and played footie until it got dark. We didn't talk about girls or the party until we went off to get some chips.

Then Zac said, "That school disco was rubbish last night." It was the first time he'd admitted this. "I was so bored."

"You laughed a lot," I said.

"Well, I'm a very good actor," Zac said. "And I thought – give the party a chance to get started – but it never did. You know what we need?"

"No," I said.

"Some great new friends."

I smiled. "There should be a shop. 'Have you got three new friends for me please? Any size and no need to wrap them.'"

Zac grinned, then looked serious again. "I'll get us some."

"How?" I asked.

"I'll sort it out when I get back," he said.

Zac is off on holiday with his parents tomorrow. And they're going to exactly the same place as last year. "It's so boring I know I'll die after one day there," said Zac with a loud sigh. "But see you in a week, Spencer.

And then get ready to make tons of new friends."

Sunday July 26th

9.05 a.m.

I dreamt that Emily called round my house. I woke up feeling really happy – for about four seconds. Now I am already overcome with sadness.

Monday July 27th

6.00 p.m.

My voice is acting so oddly. One second it's deep, the next it goes all high and squeaky. My parents tell me my voice must be breaking. Yet another horror of being a teenager.

Tuesday July 28th

7.45 p.m.

Mum has just asked me, "So where's Emily tonight?"

"I expect she's out with her boyfriend," I reply.

Mum stands there, looking like a burst balloon. "Oh, dear," she says at last.

Wednesday July 29th

8.00 p.m.

I was sitting in the lounge waiting for the football match to start on TV, when Mum burst in and switched the TV off. "Your dad wants to have a word with you, love," she said and then she half-pushed Dad into the room and left.

Dad came and sat next to me on the couch. He rubbed his hands together and said, "Well, I hear you've been having a little bit of girl trouble."

I started to go bright red. "Not really."

"Ah," he didn't say anything for a moment. His face looked very red too. Then he started again. "Didn't Emily ... er ...er," he began.

"Yes," I said, "she did."

Dad chewed his bottom lip. "Not an easy time ... do you remember when you got your first bike?" he asked.

I grinned. "Oh, yeah."

"Well, you fell off that bike at first, didn't you? But what did I tell you to do?"

"Get right back up again," I said.

Dad nodded. "That's right … well that advice doesn't just apply to bikes but many other things too. If you've had a set-back, get up and try again. Do you see?"

I nodded.

"Well done. Is there anything else you'd like to talk about?" he asked.

"No thanks," I say.

"Good lad," said Dad. "Now, what time does the football start?"

Saturday August 1st

9.45 p.m.

I have just sorted out my hundreds of comics into date order. This was an important job which needed to be done. But if I'd gone out with Emily tonight, I wouldn't have done it. So I'm very happy I don't have a girl-friend.

I don't ever plan to have one. Girls are just not worth all the bother. All they ever do is mess up your head. I'm pleased that I have found this out so early in my life. It will save me a lot of time later.

Chapter 5
Zac's New Friends

Monday August 3rd

4.05 p.m.

Zac has rung me. He's just back from holiday and tells me he has made twenty-five new friends. I laugh – he must be joking, but he says, "No, I really have. Come round and I'll tell you all about it."

9.15 p.m.

Just back from Zac's house. He says there was nothing to do on holiday – and he hated every second. Then he met this boy called

Jimmy, who told him about all the friends he'd made on Facebook. Jimmy said, "Even when I'm yawning at my parents, I can also be talking to a mate on Facebook. It's brilliant."

So now Zac is on Facebook too. Zac said, "It's dead easy. All you have to do is sign up with your details. Then you put up some pictures and say a bit about yourself such as your hobbies, etc. Then other people ask to sign up as your friend, and you can either accept or reject them. Of course, I accepted all Jimmy's best mates and they're all my best mates now. And guess what, there's one called Marc. He only lives a few miles away from here. What about that?"

Then Zac started showing me all his new Facebook friends. After each one he said things like, "Now he's totally brilliant," and, "He makes me LOL."

"What's LOL?" I asked.

Zac looked at me sadly. "Oh, Spencer, I thought everyone on the planet knew. LOL means 'laugh out loud'."

Zac went on, "I don't know why I didn't do this before. It's the most amazing thing that's ever happened to me. And it means I needn't bother about any of the people at our school any more – apart from you, of course. For now I've made real friends, who are far better than any one I know – apart from you, of course."

Tuesday August 4th

9.05 p.m.

Zac has now made 41 new friends. He says he never knew he was so popular.

9.45 p.m.

He's just texted to say it's 43 now.

Wednesday August 5th

8.00 p.m.

Zac had to get his hair cut. So he asked all his Facebook friends what hair cut to get – and got over 30 replies. "Everyone's so keen to help," he said.

"But why didn't you just ask me?" I said, a bit hurt.

Thursday August 6th

7.00 p.m.

Zac now has over 60 new friends. Every hour seems to bring a new friend for him. And he still wants more of them. I think he is going mad. And I don't know what to do about it.

Friday August 7th

6.00 p.m.

Tonight I asked my parents what they thought about Zac and all his Facebook friends. Do you know what they said? "Would you like to go on Facebook as well?"

I said, very firmly, "No I wouldn't." But they kept on and on about it. Why are teenagers always being pushed into things they don't want to do – like spending money on stupid clothes, having to go to awful parties – and now talking to people on Facebook they've never even met?

Well, I can't waste my evenings chatting to total strangers. I'm far too busy. Like tonight, there's a major TV programme on about killer whales. I've been looking forward to it all week. So has Zac, actually.

9.50 p.m.

For 90 minutes I floated right away from my life and watched killer whales in action. Totally fantastic.

The second the programme had finished, I rang Zac and then got the shock of my life. Zac had forgotten to watch it. He was too busy talking to his new friends – he's got 75 of them now. In fact, he hardly even had time to speak to me.

My bedroom suddenly seems very sad and lonely. It's horrible when you've got no one to share killer whales with.

Saturday August 8th

10.15 a.m.

My grand-parents have come for a visit. The first thing they say is how much I've grown. Then Grandad asks me if I've got a girl-friend yet. He's sort of joking. But I hear Mum say to him in the kitchen, "There was a girl he liked called Emily. She seemed such a nice girl but it didn't work out."

Nan goes, "Aaah." Then Mum starts saying how my voice was breaking. This is private information. But Mum blabs it out. Nothing's private any more.

Later Nan says to me. "Oh, Spencer, you're changing so fast I hardly know you."

"But I'm not," I begin. Only at that moment my voice goes all high and squeaky. Nan smiles at me in a highly annoying way.

Sunday August 9th

7.00 p.m.

I'm going round to Zac's house with a fantastic colour booklet called *Killers from the Sea*. It cost me £5.95. I've hardly any money left now. But if it brings Zac to his senses it will be worth it.

9.45 p.m.

Zac hardly even looked at *Killers from the Sea*. He just mumbled, "Oh, yeah, thanks," and that was it. He was too busy going on about his new girl-friend! He showed me her picture.

She has blonde hair and is, I must admit, very beautiful.

"She is, without doubt," he said, "the hottest girl I've ever met."

"Except, you haven't actually met her," I said.

Zac shook his head. "You don't get it, do you? This is how you get to know new people now. And it's so much better than meeting girls at parties. Her name's Sarah," he went on, "and she and I have been talking away for hours. Then tonight I asked her if she'd like to go out with me. And she said she would ... Are you happy for me?"

I gulped. "But, Zac, you don't know anything about her," I said.

"I know more about her than any girl at our school," he told me. Then he added, "I can find you a girl too, if you like."

"No thanks," I said at once.

Zac frowned. "I'm worried about you."

"Why?" I asked.

"If you're not careful you're going to be left behind."

"Good," I say.

"I don't think there's a teenager in Britain who doesn't have Facebook – apart from you."

"And that suits me fine," I said, "because I'm an (Un)teenager and proud of it." Then I left and took *Killers from the Sea* back with me.

Monday August 10th

Zac hasn't phoned me today and I haven't rung him. We've sort of fallen out. He didn't like me making comments about his new girl-friend. And I didn't like him saying I'm being left behind – and he didn't even look at the *Killers from the Sea* colour booklet.

Tuesday August 11th

Zac rang me – but just to say he's got 103 friends now. "They're taking up a lot of time," he said. "So this is just to let you know I'm not sure when I'll see you next."

"All right," I replied, but Zac had already rung off.

Wednesday August 12th

3.30 p.m.

Something odd has just happened. I was getting a few things at the shops for Mum when I saw Jade. I was sure she'd ignore me and I didn't want to speak to her much. But she called out, "Hi" – and after a bit – "Spencer."

"Hello," I said. I thought she'd speed past.

But she asked, "So how are you?"

"I'm fine," I said.

"Have you still ... got all your comics?"

"I put them in date order last week," I said.

"Oh, wow," she cried. "I bet you enjoyed doing that didn't you?"

I stared at her. "Why are you asking me all these questions?"

"No reason," she said, "I just thought we'd have a little chat."

"We've never had one before," I said.

"Well, we are having one now," she snapped. Then her voice went soft again. "Oh, yeah, you might give Emily a ring sometime."

"Really?" this was getting weirder and weirder.

"Yeah," said Jade, "she'd like to hear from you. "Well, see you then ... Spencer."

So what did that all mean? I tell you, girls really do mess your head up. I mean, Emily hardly spoke to me at the party. And next day when I called at her house she got Jade to say she was ill. And then I saw her walking up the road with that smelly, stinking Oscar – and a drippy expression on her face.

Yet, now Jade tells me to ring Emily.

Should I?

5.30 p.m.

I'd like to ring Zac and ask him what to do. But he'll probably be busy with his 103 virtual friends. And it's too embarrassing to talk about with my parents.

WHAT SHOULD I DO?

9.00 p.m.

I nearly ring Emily but in the end, I don't. I am still too upset and shaken.

9.05 p.m.

And anyway, why couldn't Emily ring me?

10.35 p.m.

Still thinking about Emily. I'm glad I didn't call her. Girls are nothing but trouble. Also, my feelings for Emily are cooling off – or they will be soon, I hope.

Thursday August 13th

3.30 p.m.

Another surprise – but a good one. Zac has just phoned me. He now has over 120 friends but he still wants us to be mates.

"You'll be one mate I'll never turn my back on," he says. "You can't help being a geeky nerd," he adds. "I was just like you once."

Then he asks me to go round his house right away. "I've got some really exciting news for you," he says.

Chapter 6
Party Time

Friday August 14th

9.15 p.m.

Just back from Zac's house. His really exciting news is that he has been invited to a party by Marc. "You remember Marc," he cried, "the guy on Facebook who lives near here. He's one of my very best mates."

"Oh, yeah," I said.

"Marc's having a summer party and guess who else is going? Sarah, my new girl-friend.

I'm going to meet her for the very first time at Marc's party. What about that?"

"I'm really pleased for you," I said.

"Guess who else is going?" he asked.

I gave a shrug.

"I've got another invite for ... you," he said with a big grin.

"Me?" I was amazed.

"Yeah, it'll be good for you to meet some new girls."

"No thank you," I said. Then I told him about my odd chat with Jade.

"How interesting," he said. "Still, you were right not to ring Emily. Let her call you."

"Do you think she will?" I asked at once.

Zac gave a shrug. "Anyway, you'll meet tons of girls at this party."

"No thanks," I said.

Zac looked shocked. "But you've got to come ... I need you there."

"No you don't," I said. "You've got Marc and Sarah and ..."

"Oh, I know they're top people," he told me, "but I don't want to walk in there on my own. So come with me."

"You know I don't like parties," I said firmly.

"You'll like this one," he said.

"No I won't," I said. "I'm just not a party person."

"Do it as a massive favour for me," said Zac.

I hesitated.

Zac smiled. "Thanks a million."

"I haven't said yes, yet," I said.

"Yes you have ... and there's one more massive favour I need you to do for me."

9.40 p.m.

I opened my wardrobe door – and pulled out the hoodie. This was Zac's other massive favour. He wants me to wear this to the party.

"Look on it as fancy dress," he said. And just for one night you're dressing as a teenager."

To wear such an ugly thing is a real test of friendship. I gulp hard and then looked at my orange knitted jumper and matching knitted tie. That is so much smarter than a hoodie. Why am I the only teenager who can see that?

10.15 p.m.

Emily hasn't rung. I haven't been waiting for her to call. But these are the facts.

Saturday August 15th

6.00 p.m.

I was just putting on the dreaded hoodie when Zac called round. My dad's giving us a lift to the party but Zac was very early. I sensed he had something important to tell me.

Zac started to walk around my bedroom. "When you meet Sarah, my girl-friend, tonight – well, she knows I like footie. But she also thinks I'm in the school team ... well, I was nearly picked, wasn't I?"

I nodded.

"And she thinks I'm the school team's star player."

"All right," I say.

"She also thinks I had a trial for Chelsea last week."

"What?" I cried.

"Yeah, got a little bit carried away there. But she was dead impressed. I also go mountain climbing a lot. And oh, yeah – once I helped you."

"What did you do?" I asked.

"Oh, nothing much really – just saved your life. You'd been swimming and went out too far. So I had to rescue you."

"You're a champion swimmer I suppose," I said.

"I've won six cups, yeah," Zac said.

"What about if she wants to see them?" I asked.

"I'll have to say I keep them all in my uncle's castle."

"You've got an uncle with a castle?"

"Oh, yeah. And I told her I'm going to be in a film soon."

I started to laugh.

"It's not funny," he said. "I didn't mean to make up all this stuff. But I'm going out with an amazingly hot girl. So I've got to try and impress her. And it doesn't feel like you're lying, when you say it on the internet. You're just trying on a new image. You even start to believe it yourself. So don't let me down, will you?"

"I'll just nod at everything you say," I told him.

"I will tell her the truth," said Zac, "one day. Well come on, let's split."

I took one last look round my bedroom. It always seems extra friendly when I'm leaving it to go to school discos or parties.

6.15 p.m.

Downstairs Mum and Dad were waiting for us.

"I'm only wearing this hoodie and these other vile clothes once," I told them. "Never again."

Mum and Dad nodded but I'm not sure they believed me.

7.40 p.m.

Dad drove us to Marc's house. Dad had called Marc's dad so he knew where the party was. But it wasn't very hard to find. Outside the house balloons were hanging from the windows and you could hear the music pounding away.

"Why must the music be so loud?" I said. "It makes good talk really difficult."

Zac looked at me. "Promise me you won't say anything else like that tonight."

"I'm just telling you what I think," I said.

"Well don't ... you'll spoil everything."

Zac and I got out of the car. I told Dad we'd ring him by half past ten at the latest to pick us up.

"Get ready for a brilliant night," said Zac to me.

He rang on the doorbell. Through the glass door I could see lots of shapes rushing about. Then the door was opened a tiny bit – and looming over us was this huge boy with a broken nose.

"Yeah," he said.

"We've come for the party. Marc invited us. I'm Zac." The huge boy peered down at us and then yelled out. "Marc, there's a geezer here who reckons he knows you. He's called Zac."

There was a long wait before a boy with curly dark hair came to the door looking very puzzled. "Who are you?" he asked.

"I'm Zac."

He still looked puzzled.

"We met on Facebook."

Another long silence.

In fact, I was getting ready to leave when at last the boy yelled, "Oh, Zac," he raised his hand. "Hey, buddy, give me five."

"And this is my mate, Spencer," said Zac. "I told you he was coming too."

And I had to give Marc five too.

"Well, brilliant to see you both," said Marc to us.

"Yeah, really good," agreed Zac.

"Fantastic," I added.

We were allowed inside the party. Then the boy at the door, who was Marc's cousin and was called Kyle, thundered at us, "Shoes!"

Marc told us "Yeah, we're asking everyone to take off their shoes. Just chuck them anywhere."

"But I need mine back," I began, "because they were a present from ..." I stopped because I could feel Zac looking hard at me. I didn't say anything else.

"Well, guys," Marc said, "there's food and drink in the kitchen, and you'll know tons of people here."

"I'm meeting Sarah here, actually," said Zac.

"Sarah?" said Marc, looking puzzled.

"Yeah, I met her on Facebook too. And now we're going out together."

"Hey, wicked," said Marc. "I do know her but I haven't met her yet. So it's cool she's coming tonight. Well, catch you later."

"Yeah, great," said Zac.

After Marc had darted away, Zac said, "What a top guy, a friend for life. And what a great buzz. Let's party."

"If you go upstairs you'll be chucked out," shouted Kyle after us. "And no alcohol."

Kyle really knew how to make you feel welcome.

The house was packed full of teenagers who just seemed to keep moving about. We fought our way into the kitchen. But all the food had gone. We just grabbed beakers of flat lemonade.

The kitchen smelt of cheesy feet and perfume, mixed with hair-spray and sick. Yes, someone had been sick already. And two adults, who I guessed were Marc's parents, suddenly came in and cleared up the mess. They also told off a group of boys for breaking a glass.

"All right, don't go loopy about one little glass," one of the boys muttered. "It probably only cost you about four pence. And this is supposed to be a party." Then all three of the boys charged off.

"Hope they're not some of your Facebook friends," I said to Zac.

But Zac hardly even saw them. He was too excited. "Here we are, right inside the action," he said. "Isn't this a great feeling, Spencer?"

I did my best to look keen, as someone's armpit squashed against my face.

"We ought to go and get stuck in," said Zac. "I've got so many mates here ... And we've got to find Sarah of course. That's number one priority."

8.20 p.m.

We have just found Sarah, only things haven't turned out at all as we'd expected.

Chapter 7
The Real Sarah

8.21 p.m.

Zac and I were squashed together in the kitchen, with Zac keeping this funny little smile on his face all the time. And then this girl came up to us. "You're not Zac, are you?" she said.

"That's right," said Zac.

"Well, I'm Sarah," the girl said.

Zac nearly fell over with shock and I was pretty stunned myself. For Sarah didn't look anything like the girl on Facebook, who had blonde hair and was really beautiful. This Sarah had dark brown hair. She wasn't ugly, but she was totally different to her picture.

"Zac," said Zac. "Never heard of the guy … and now I've got to go to the loo. Bye."

He ran off and I was left with Sarah. "That was Zac, wasn't it?" she said softly.

"Er well … I think so," I said.

"I know I shouldn't have done it," she said.

"Done what?" I asked.

"Well, all the photos of me are awful. So when I went on Facebook, I stuck up a picture of my cousin instead. People do say we look at bit alike."

"Do they?" I said.

"Oh, who am I kidding? I'm a big let-down and now Zac will never want to talk to me again." Tears welled up in her eyes.

"Oh, no," I said quickly. "Zac only went off so fast because … because he's got the runs – in and out of the loo all evening, poor guy. I'll just go and get him now."

I rushed off to find Zac. I couldn't see him anywhere. Then I spotted him standing on the patio in the garden. Hardly anyone else was outside, just those three boys who'd been told off. They were all crowded on one garden swing, until Kyle yelled at them to get off before they broke it.

"Zac, what are you doing out here?" I asked.

He span round. "Well you saw her. She's having a laugh, isn't she? She looks nothing like her picture."

"She didn't like any of the photos of herself," I told him, "so she put one of her cousin up instead."

"What a cheek," said Zac. "Well, I'm never talking to her again."

"Oh, you can't just leave her," I said.

"Yes I can. You either press accept or reject. And I'm pressing reject."

"You might do that on the internet," I said, "but not in real life. Come on, give her a chance."

"No," said Zac.

"But she's your girl-friend. You could at least talk to her."

"I've just got one word to say to her," said Zac. "Good-bye."

"She is quite pretty," I said.

"Quite pretty," said Zac. "Sarah was lush."

"Well, maybe she won't mind too much when she finds out you didn't really have a trial for Chelsea or make a film. Come on, you've got to speak to her."

We went back inside. Sarah was still in the kitchen looking more sad than ever.

I gave Zac a little push. "Go on, she's waiting for you."

"Stop bossing me about," muttered Zac. "I'm only going to ask her for her cousin's phone number." He started walking over to Sarah, and then he stopped and said. "By the way, Spencer, guess who else is at this party?"

"Who?" I asked.

"Emily," he said, with a big grin.

Before I could ask any more questions he'd gone.

Chapter 8
Something Terrible

Saturday August 15th

8.30 p.m.

That was a shock. That Emily was here – of all places. And yes, I do want to see her again – and find out why she wanted me to ring her. Of course I shan't go looking for Emily – I'll just walk around this party until I bump into her by accident.

8.40 p.m.

Just found out who else is here – Oscar. He and Emily have come together, of course. I should have guessed that. Feel totally crushed now.

9.05 p.m.

Get ready to be very shocked, dear diary, as I have let myself down very badly.

I rushed around the party trying to find Zac. I wanted to tell him I couldn't stay at this party another second and I was going. But more and more people were arriving and it was impossible to move anywhere. In the end I pushed my way into the garden.

My head was spinning. I was so angry and hurt that I didn't know what I was doing. It is very important you remember that.

Anyway, three boys were outside. The boys who'd been in trouble earlier. They had found some golf balls now and they were throwing these onto the next-door's roof. One must have hit the roof because they let out a massive cheer.

Normally I'd have just ignored them. But tonight I felt so odd that ... I really don't want to say what I did next. But I must.

One golf ball was left. I rushed up and grabbed it. One of them called out, "Leave it!" But that didn't stop me. I was so worked up I hurled that golf ball right into the air, didn't I?

I missed the roof of course. I'm a terrible shot. But just then there was a great roar like a rhino in a very bad mood. I span round and there was Kyle thundering towards us. And he had Marc's parents and Marc right behind him.

"You lot again!" he yelled at the three boys. "You're nothing but trouble!"

"I want you all to leave now!" screeched Marc's mum.

"You heard," yelled Kyle, "out now – all of you!"

It was only then I worked out he thought I was one of the gang. And I was being chucked out of a party. "But look, I'm not with them ..." I began.

"Move!" yelled Kyle.

"Look, everyone, just chill ..." one of the boys started to call out.

But his voice fell away as Kyle got closer. And us four "trouble-makers" had to leave by the back gate.

A crowd came out to watch our walk of shame. Zac was there too and he just stared and stared at me, as if he were dreaming. He even rubbed his eyes.

The back gate swung open. "Don't try and come back!" shouted Kyle. The three boys didn't argue until they were outside. Then they yelled about what a rubbish party it had been – and they said some more words which I won't repeat.

I thought I should leave in a more polite way so I called over to Marc. "Thank you very much for inviting me. And I hope the rest of the party goes well for you." But Marc didn't answer, just frowned at me with his arms folded.

Then I said to Kyle. "Er, excuse me, but what about my shoes?"

"You should have thought about that before," he snapped and then pushed me outside. Then he slammed the gate shut and locked it.

And I stood there with no shoes – and no pride.

9.25 p.m.

Zac has just dashed out of the party and over to me. "Why were you hanging about with those guys?" he asked.

"I wasn't with them," I said. "It's just they were throwing golf balls about – and I threw one too."

Zac stepped back from me. "But why?"

I shook my head.

"I don't understand," said Zac. "I mean, you've never done anything like that before. Come on, tell me. What's wrong?"

"I was angry," I said, at last.

"About what?"

"Well, Emily is here. But so is Oscar. They've come together. And knowing that made me mad with fury."

Zac burst out laughing.

"What's funny?" I asked.

"You are," he said. "Look, don't move."

"I can't exactly go far," I said. "I'm standing here in my socks."

"I'll go back into the party and sort this out," said Zac.

9.40 p.m.

Only Zac couldn't get back into the party.

"That bone-head, Kyle, wouldn't let me back in," he told me. "So then I asked to see Marc. But he didn't want to know. He looked right through me – great mate he is."

"What about Sarah?" I asked.

"Well, we'd just got chatting when you started throwing golf balls about."

I hung my head.

"But look who's coming our way," said Zac.

I looked up. It was Emily.

Chapter 9
Emily Tells All

9.58 p.m.

I have just spoken to Emily for a whole seven minutes. At first she did most of the talking.

"Oh, Spencer," she said, "what a mess. I'm so sorry. Look, I didn't come here with Oscar tonight. I came to this party for just one reason – to see you. Do you believe that?"

"Yes, OK," I croaked.

"Zac told me you would be here. And that it was up to me to sort all this mess out."

"Zac did?" I cried.

So that's why he was so keen for me to come to this party. Zac was now being highly tactful and standing a little way from us.

"But you have been going out with Oscar, haven't you?" I cried.

"Look, will you just let me explain?" she cried. She sounded really worked up.

"Yes, all right," I said.

"Oscar said he liked me. And a lot of girls really rate him. So when he asked me out all the girls said I should go."

"Including Jade," I said.

"Most of all Jade," she grinned. "I didn't want to go out with Oscar because he's not my type. But Jade said if I didn't, everyone would call me 'chicken' and no one would like me. So I said I'd meet him at the school disco. Only at the last minute I told Oscar I felt ill and had to go home."

"Jade said you left the party early because you didn't like what I was wearing."

"Oh, no," she cried. "She just made that up because ..."

"Because she thinks I'm weird," I interrupted.

"Because she really wanted me to go out with Oscar," said Emily.

"But Oscar did go round your house the next day. I saw him ... not that I've been stalking you or anything," I added. "I just happened to see him."

"Yes, Oscar did come round to see how I was," said Emily. "And then he took me to this café round the corner. And I told him that I didn't want to go out with him. I tried to be nice about it. He was all right about it in the end. But it's been such a muddle. Then I really was ill for quite a few days actually." She stopped, and then she said softly, "But one night I watched this programme on killer whales."

"You saw that?" I said. I was so excited. She nodded.

"And while I was watching those killer whales I couldn't stop thinking about you," she said.

I blushed at this huge compliment.

She went on. "I was missing you so much. Jade saw and felt bad for pushing me at Oscar. That's why Jade asked you to ring me. But it was up to me to sort things out – not you. And that's all I've got to say really."

We smiled at each other then, not sure what to say next. At last I said, "That killer whale programme is the first of four, you know. There's another one on next week. It should be even better."

"Oh, excellent," Emily said eagerly.

Then I burst out, "So would you care to watch it round my house?" And for the second time that night I shocked myself. For I was asking Emily to see me in the middle of a week, not on a Saturday. And normally I like to watch shows on killer whales all by myself, so I can really focus on them.

"I'd love to – but do me a favour, don't wear those clothes you've got on."

"You don't like them," I said.

"Well, they're just not you, are they?"

"They're really not," I agreed.

I think we'd have kissed then – only Zac came over with Sarah. So instead, Emily's arm just brushed against mine for a moment, and I squeezed it tightly.

10.15 p.m.

Emily's gone now. Her dad has just picked her up. Sarah has left too. But Zac thinks he will see her again.

"And does she know you haven't made a film or had a trial for Chelsea?" I asked.

"Not yet," he admitted. "I'm sort of her dream boyfriend right now. So I can't just smash all those dreams, can I?" Then he quickly changed the subject. "So what about Emily, then?"

"Thanks very much for phoning her," I said.

"What are mates for?" said Zac. "Real mates."

And now here's my dad's car. And I shall have to tell him why I don't have any shoes. This would normally worry me greatly. But right now it really doesn't. I'm just too happy. Because next Tuesday evening I'm going to watch killer whales with Emily.

Can life get any better?

Barrington Stoke would like to thank all its readers for commenting on the manuscript before publication and in particular:

Jenny Allen

Vanessa Barnauskaite

Kieran Cheal

Sarah Collinge

George Domyanov

Goodness Duru

Hannah Eggington

Nathan Gillett

Benjamin Greaves

Thomas Green

Rebecca Hadland

Nikki Heath

Benjamin Humphries

Kalenga Mumba

Olivia Rutkowska

Jack West

Become a Consultant!

Would you like to be a consultant? Ask your parent, carer or teacher to contact us at the email address below – we'd love to hear from them! They can also find out more by visiting our website.

schools@barringtonstoke.co.uk
www.barringtonstoke.co.uk